For Kurin,

Much love,

Many stories.

[signature] 2013

Scarlet Says Good-Bye

A story I read with _____

For my beloved husband Matt—
Build me a boat that can carry two,
And both shall row, my true love and I.
Traditional

With special thanks to the UnitedHealth Group
Innovation Council for their support and commitment to
helping children and families in times of need.

Hardcover: ISBN: 978-0-9847622-3-1
Library of Congress Control Number: 2012936262

First Printing: April 2012
16 15 14 13   5 4 3 2
United Healthcare Services, Inc.
Minneapolis, Minnesota 55413
Printed in the United States

Scarlet Says Good-Bye

By Christine L. Thompson

Illustration by Hillary Hempstead

Art Direction by Michael Ringler

Dear Friend,

Right now is a very sad time for your family. We are thinking of you.

We wrote this book because we wanted you to spend time with your loved one. They're in hospice care because they are dying, and this book contains a story and activities you can do with your family - or by yourself - to help you remember the person you care about, and the time you spent with them.

Your loved one will always be in your heart, and it is important to remember that the person you love loves you, too.

Take care,
Your friends at UnitedHealthcare

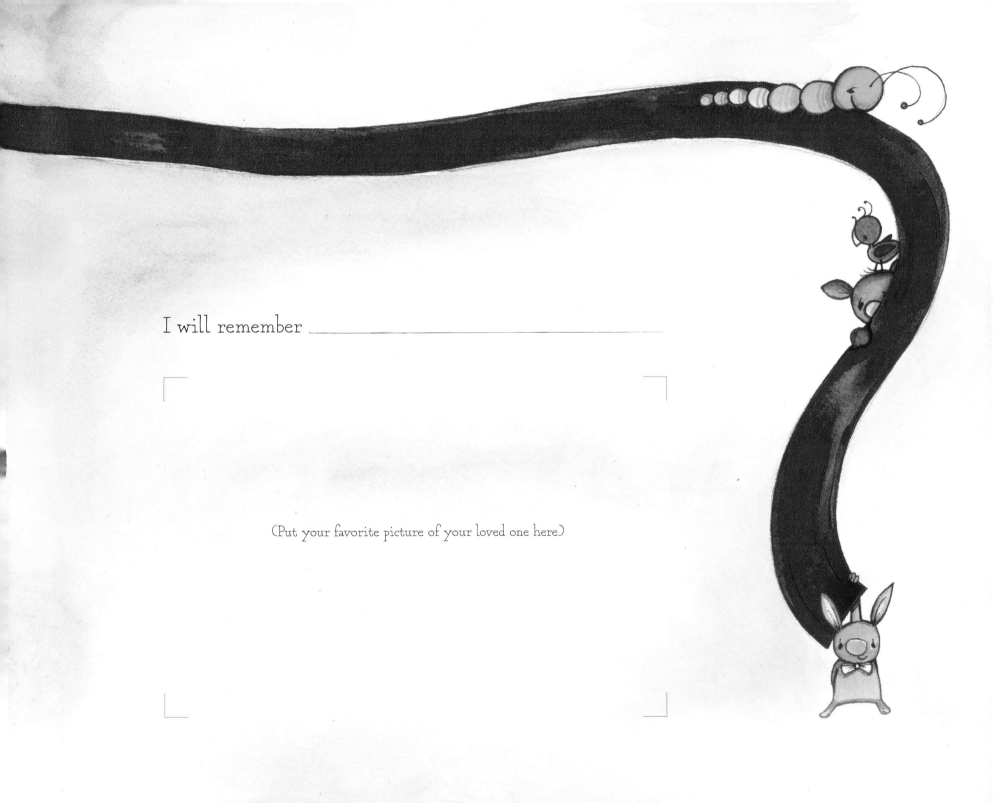

I will remember _____

(Put your favorite picture of your loved one here)

Scarlet Says Good-Bye
a hospice story

"Will you tell me a story?" Scarlet asks.
"Yes Scarlet. Here is a story about me."

When I was young I didn't know why
Time would go fast when it was my time to die.

"When you were little like me, what did you like to do?"

I played with my friends and climbed lots of trees,
I read many books and swam in the sea.
I learned many things and—strange as it seems—
I had great adventures in all of my dreams.

Then came the day when I got so sick.
I did what I could but it could not be fixed.

"But why can't the doctors fix you?"

The doctors have tried as hard as they can.
But nothing can make me healthy again.

"I heard Mom say that you are going to hospice.
Where is hospice?" Scarlet asks.

"Hospice isn't a place, Scarlet, it's some very special people
and how they will care for me. Let's finish our story."

I wanted no pain and I wanted to rest.
The hospice help came and they were the best.
They heard all my stories and met all my wishes,
they helped ease my pain... and even washed dishes.

I knew what I needed and let hospice know, too.

They helped my whole family and they can help you.

"But why is everyone so sad?"

It's my time to die. I am so weak.
My heartbeat is faint. I can barely speak.
But all of my family is standing right here.
There is so much love, I have no fear.

Now I am at peace. It's my time to die.

I hope, my dear Scarlet, now you know why.

With Love,

_____

My wish for you is _____

_____

Games and Other Things

Some good things to know.

Children-

It is important to know that all of your feelings are okay; you cannot control how you feel. But, you can control how you express your feelings and there are healthy ways to act even when you feel sad, afraid, angry or lonely.

Some things that may help you express your emotions are:
- talking with someone you trust
- listening or playing some music
- making art (like drawing or crafts)
- playing, on your own or with some friends
- creating a Memory Box and filling it with pictures, drawings and keepsakes to help you remember your favorite things about your loved one. Decorate it and add messages or stories.

Just like you, the adults in your life are grieving. Always know that you are loved, safe and cared for. You have adults in your life to support you when you have questions or want to share your feelings.

Remember that the memories and love that you shared with your special person are forever, nothing can ever take them away.

Parents- (Adults)

Here are some simple guidelines to keep in mind as you support your grieving child.
- Teach that death is a part of life.
- Encourage questions. Be simple and honest when answering them.
- Recognize and acknowledge all feelings.
- In addition to verbal communication, provide additional outlets for expression of feelings (for example art, music, play).
- Understand the developmental stages of grieving (see Resources page).
- Be a positive role model. Let children observe you grieving in a healthy way.
- Listen and love unconditionally.

In support as you journey through grief,
Sarah Kroenke, BSSW, LSW Park Nicollet Methodist Hospice: Growing through Grief Social Worker and
Program Coordinator, sarah.kroenke@parknicollet.com

Unscramble the words below.

1. ecpea _____   10. grnaci _____

2. htosplai _____   11. elvo _____

3. ylafim _____   12. usnre _____

4. abtehaetr _____

5. pcosieh _____

6. esmioerm _____

7. oodtcr _____

8. daemrs _____

9. aisgrnh _____

Can you find...

9 balloons
5 birds
A pair of flippers
A spider
A crayon
3 bunnies
Eyeglasses

A treasure chest
A baseball
Scarlet's scarf
A heart
A snail
5 ladybugs
A glass of lemonade

Color Elby and his friends.

Help Elby and friends find Scarlet's scarf.

Pretend you're a reporter asking some questions to your loved one.
Write his or her answers here.

When you were little...

Where did you live? _____

Did you get in trouble? _____

Did you have any pets? _____

What were their names? _____

Who was your best friend? _____

What was your favorite movie? _____

Did you have a favorite toy? _____

Did you like school? _____

What was your favorite subject or teacher? _____

Did you play sports? _____

Now that you're big...

What is your favorite thing to do? _____

What is your favorite food? _____

What is your favorite memory of me? _____

_____

Who is your favorite superhero? _____

What was your first job? _____

What is your favorite movie? _____

What is your favorite color? _____

What is your happiest memory? _____

_____

My journal. This is a place to write down your
thoughts or feelings.

My favorite pictures.

My favorite memory with you.

(Draw it and tell the story).

Connect the dots and color.

What would you like to say to your loved one
before he or she dies?

Dear _____ ,

_____
_____
_____
_____
_____
_____
_____
_____
_____
_____
_____
_____

Love,

Color Scarlet's world.

Draw a picture of the people you love.

Find some friends to play along!

Find the words listed below and then see if you
can find words or pictures or both in the book.

C U R K N P G W I Z G Y C B S D H S I F X C T F I K M F R S
   D E A W O R R P N W S A T H O W X S L W O R I L L A X E
   P R T B H F D N M L F N N K Y C C S S O Z I L V E N G S
   R A N S L P U R V A T D E V Z A T D E P A E R B V J E S
F O U I I O I B E R A N L A R W R U O O Z L T N Y X X M Z A
T B A R W N H S E U V L I I A F K G B K R P G D T S P T J L
H R E E S E T Q R E H T L D P J B A W H M J D G D V C D M G
F Z R D K E W I T O S R J I F F Z B M G H E W D O M E Q S E
J S C A R L E T N C K R C S P C L O U D T J I M V G P K E Y
G U B Y D A L D E G O P U P O R E X R A Y S C K I S A Z Y E
L N O D Z T V B E P O U P B P S E U P Z L K C H F K M I T Z
P W A Y O R O R U R B P Z V A K C T S G V D A E Q F L F U D
V L I C N E P W P L U P J V I Y J P A Z H X Q F Y E E R N V
L N C X G G X X G M K Y S S N M H B R C B A L L O O N S S Y
G A I N V O W J T K T W B F K Z Z C C C H N Y H W S Z P N Y

balloons	bunny	doctor	flowers	goggles	parents	rainbow	teddybear
bandaid	caterpillar	dog	friend	nurse	parrot	red scarf	tree
bed	cloud	eyeglasses	ladybug	owl	pencil	scarlet	vase
books	cup	fish	lamp	painting	puppy	sister	xray

Things we like to do together:

Create your own bookmark ⌄

How to draw Elby.

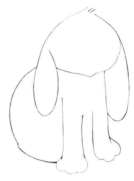

1. "Start with my head and body...

2. ... then add my ears and front legs.

3. Don't forget my back legs and collar

4. Now, lets add my nose

5. eyes and mouth.

6. And finally, my spots."

Now you try.

My journal.

Doodle, doodle, doodle!

Resources for Kids, Teens and Families.

Allina Grief Resources: www.allina.com/ahs/grief.nsf
Grief resources and information for adults and children

Center for Grieving Children: www.cgcmaine.org
Provides book lists, educational articles and helpful links

The Dougy Center: www.dougy.org
Grief resources for kids, teens and young adults

Evercare Hospice and Palliative Care: www.evercarehospice.com
Resources and information on hospice care services, answers to frequently asked questions about hospice and palliative care

Growing through Grief
A Minnesota metro-area school based support program for children and teens that are anticipating or have experienced the death of a loved one. **Contact:** SarahKroenke@sarah.kroenke@parknicollet.com

www.KidSaid.com
Online grief support for kids

Many Strong: www.ManyStrong.com
Together we're stronger. Create a community of family and friends for emotional and financial support

A Memory Book of a Loved One
A beautiful, healing journal to commemorate the life of a special person. Designed for children ages 5-12 as well as teens and adults. **Contact:** SarahKroenke@sarah.kroenke@parknicollet.com

Moyer Family Foundation: www.MoyerFoundation.org
Empowers children in distress through education and support. Operates bereavement camps for children nationwide.

To order more copies of *"Scarlet Says Good-bye"* or to share your stories and feedback, please email Christine at christine_l_thompson@uhc.com.